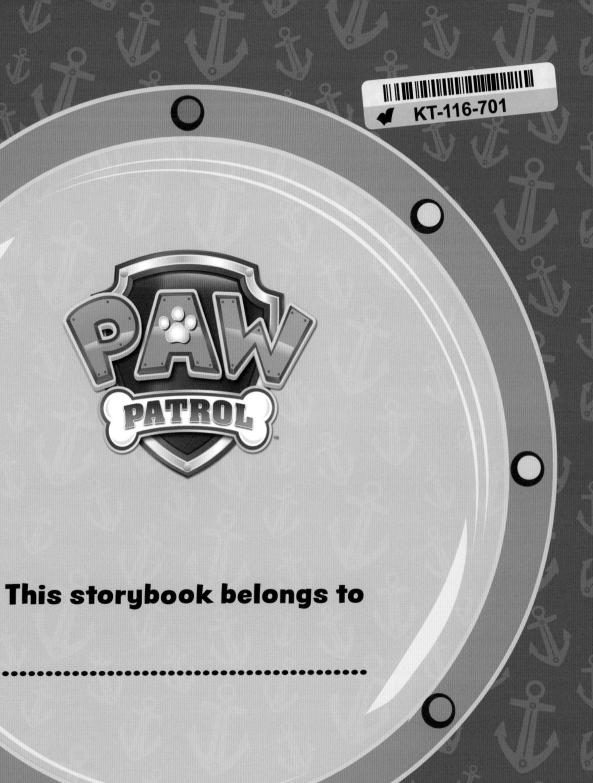

PAW PATROL

This storybook belongs to

....

First published in United States 2018 by Penguin Random House
This edition published in Great Britain 2023 by Farshore
An imprint of HarperCollins*Publishers*
1 London Bridge Street, London SE1 9GF
www.farshore.co.uk

HarperCollins*Publishers*
Macken House, 39/40 Mayor Street Upper,
Dublin 1, D01 C9W8, Ireland

ISBN 978 0 00 850095 5
Printed in the UK
001

A CIP catalogue record for this title is available from the British Library.

Stay safe online. Farshore is not responsible for content hosted by third parties.

This book is produced from independently certified FSC™ paper
to ensure responsible forest management.

For more information visit: www.harpercollins.co.uk/green

SEA PATROL TO THE RESCUE

One sunny morning, the PAW Patrol were at their new Beach Tower headquarters. Mayor Goodway had asked the pups to be Adventure Beach's new lifeguard rescue team. She wanted them on duty during her party that afternoon.

"We'll be the Sea Patrol," Ryder announced. "But before you can save anyone, you'll have to earn your lifeguard badges."

"Ready, set, get wet!" barked Zuma.

For the lifeguard test, the pups didn't rescue a person. They took turns swimming through a course of floating buoys and rescuing a pineapple named Mr Prickly! One by one, each pup earned a badge . . . until it was Rocky's turn.

"That's okay," he said. "I don't like getting wet."
"You can't be a lifeguard without getting wet," Skye said.
"Hmmm," Rocky said to himself. "We'll see about that!"

Instead of swimming, Rocky jumped from buoy to buoy, then threw a life ring around Mr Prickly. He pulled the pineapple in and hopped back to shore without getting wet!

"Cool rescue technique," Ryder said. "But if you want to earn your lifeguard badge, you have to swim." Rocky was happy to be a land guard. "I know you can do this," said Ryder. "If you don't feel up to it now, you can try again later."

Meanwhile, Cap'n Turbot was out at sea feeding Wally the Walrus. "Here's some more juicy jellyfish jerky," he said. He didn't realise that a baby octopus was stuck to the side of his bucket.

Suddenly, the water started churning and Cap'n Turbot's boat, the Flounder, began to rock. Giant tentacles reached out of the waves and wrapped around the boat. "Great gushing geysers – I need the PAW Patrol!" Cap'n Turbot exclaimed. He called Ryder for help.

Ryder told the pups about Cap'n Turbot's boat.

"The Sea Patrol is on a roll!"

"Um, Ryder, how are we going to get out to the Flounder?" Rubble asked.

Ryder pushed a button on his PupPad.

The Beach Tower shook as a huge ship called the Sea Patroller detached from it. Robo Dog was at the controls and he loaded Zuma and Rubble's special sea vehicles onto it. Ryder, Rubble, Zuma and Marshall hopped aboard and the Sea Patroller sped to the rescue.

The Sea Patroller reached the troubled Flounder. Zuma and Rubble hit the waves in their new sea vehicles.

Zuma tried to pull the tentacles off Cap'n Turbot's boat with his vehicle's mechanical arms, but the sea monster was too strong.

Ryder had an idea. He told Robo Dog to sound the Sea Patroller's horn.

BWAAAAAAAA!

The startled sea monster released the Flounder and slid back below the ocean's surface.

"Hooray!" everyone cheered.

But just then, the Flounder started to sink, with Cap'n Turbot still on board!

Rubble used his crane to pluck Cap'n Turbot off the deck – just as the boat
slipped under the waves.
"The pups and I will do everything we can to raise the Flounder," Ryder promised.
As Rubble headed back to land, no one noticed the little stowaway stuck to
Cap'n Turbot's life ring.

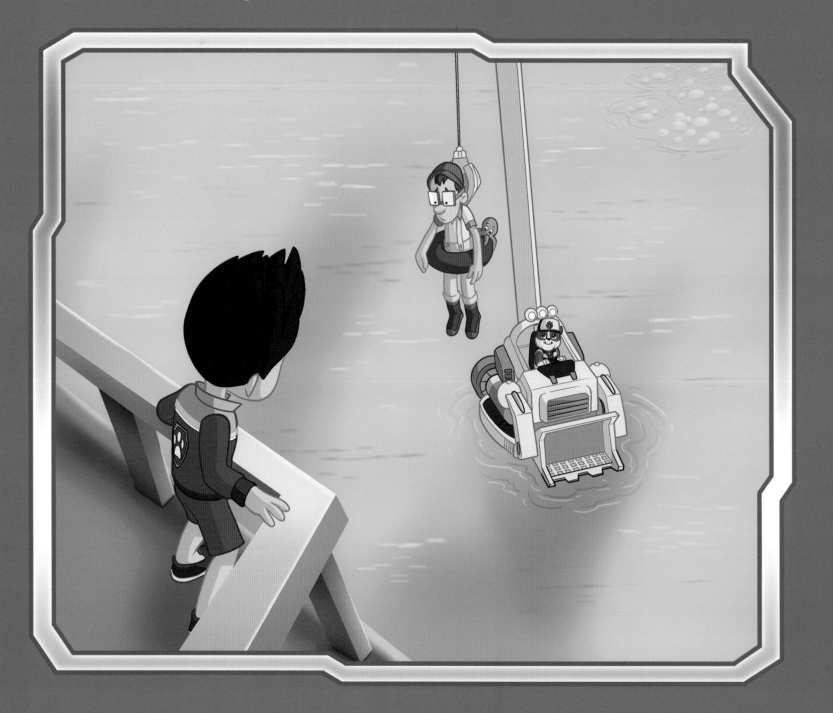

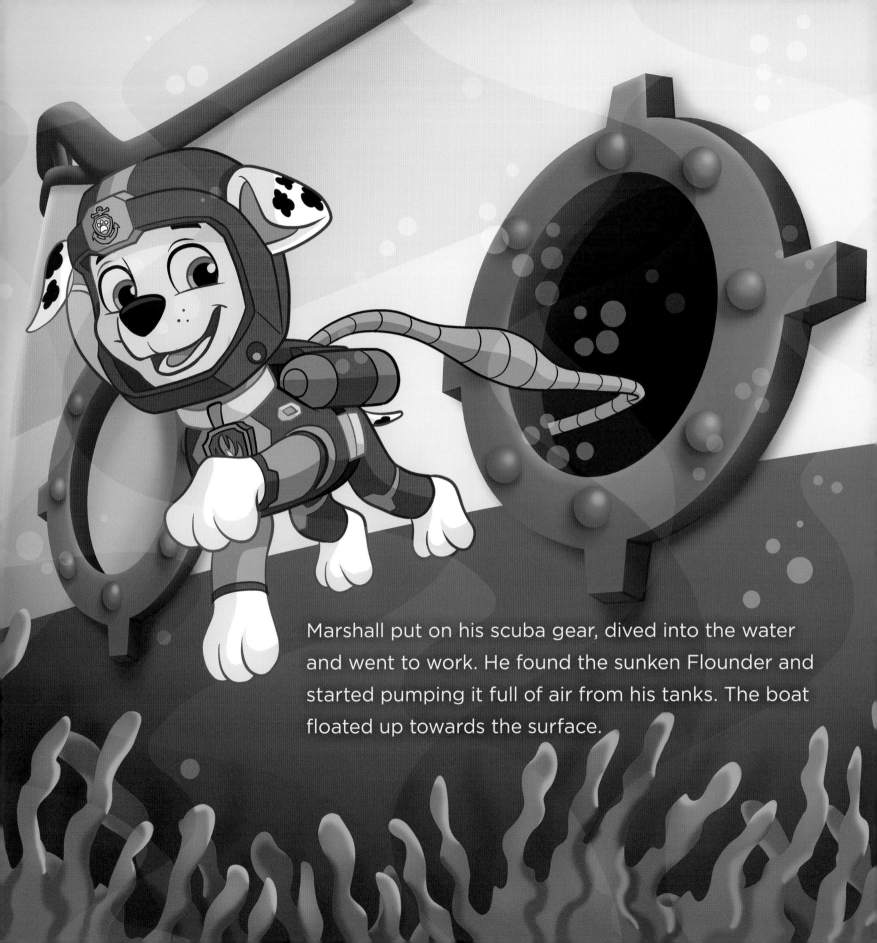

Marshall put on his scuba gear, dived into the water and went to work. He found the sunken Flounder and started pumping it full of air from his tanks. The boat floated up towards the surface.

As Marshall watched the boat rise, something shiny caught his eye.

Was it undersea treasure?

He picked it up with his mechanical claw and shook it.

"It's a baby rattle!" he exclaimed.

Meanwhile, Cap'n Turbot was back on Adventure Beach trying to cheer himself up at Mayor Goodway's party. But while he looked for something to eat, the little stowaway octopus jumped off him and landed on Mayor Humdinger's head!

"Help!" the mayor shouted. "Get it off!"

Just then, the sea monster rose out of the waves! Skye took to the air with her parasail to distract it while Rubble built a sand wall to protect the beachgoers. When Ryder arrived, he saw that the sea monster was actually an octopus – and it was squinting.

"It's looking for something, but it can't see very well."

"Well, keep it away from me," muttered Mayor Humdinger. "I don't want that on my head, too!"

Then Ryder realised the giant octopus was the little octopus's mother. "We need to get that baby back to its mum!"

But first they had to get the baby off Mayor Humdinger's head.
Marshall remembered the rattle he'd found and started shaking it.
The baby octopus reached for the toy . . . but because Mayor Humdinger
couldn't see, he accidentally knocked the rattle into the ocean!

Someone had to get that rattle!

"I can find it with my metal detector," said Rocky.

"Are you sure, Rocky?" Ryder asked. "You'll have to swim and get wet."

"If getting wet will help the baby octopus get back to its mum, I can do it!" Rocky declared. He extended his metal detector, bravely dived into the water and found the rattle!

Shaking the toy, Zuma boarded the Sea Patroller with Ryder and headed away from the beach. The little octopus followed the rattling noise . . . and the mother followed her baby. Out in the deep water, the mother and baby found each other and hugged.

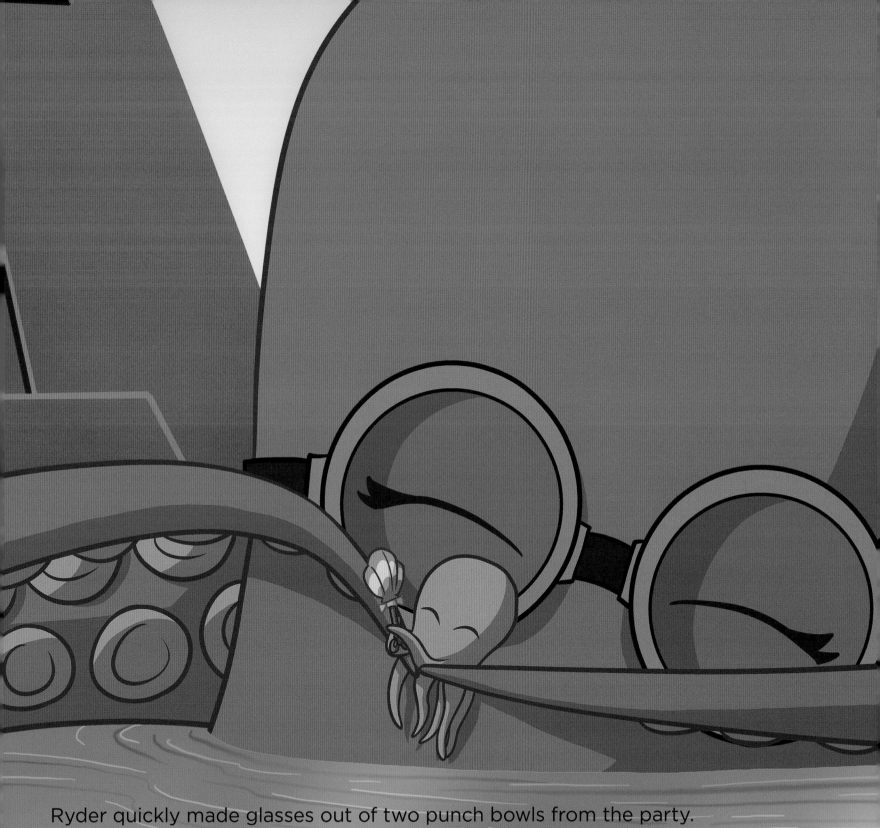

Ryder quickly made glasses out of two punch bowls from the party.
Now the mother could always find her baby. The Sea Patrol had worked
together and saved the day!

Back on the beach, everyone cheered for the pups – and for Cap'n Turbot's newly repaired Flounder.

"Thank you, PAW Patrol," said Mayor Goodway. "You saved the beach and the party!"

"I think Rocky deserves the biggest thank you," said Ryder. "He got wet to save the day and earned this." Ryder pinned a lifeguard badge to Rocky's vest. All the pups howled and hoorayed for their brave friend!

THE END

A REVVED-UP RACING ADVENTURE

Join the pit-crew **PAW Patrol** pups as they work together to keep race day on track. Meet you at the finish line! **READY, RACE, RESCUE!**

ISBN: 978-0-00-852626-9

AN ACTION-PACKED MEDIEVAL MISSION!

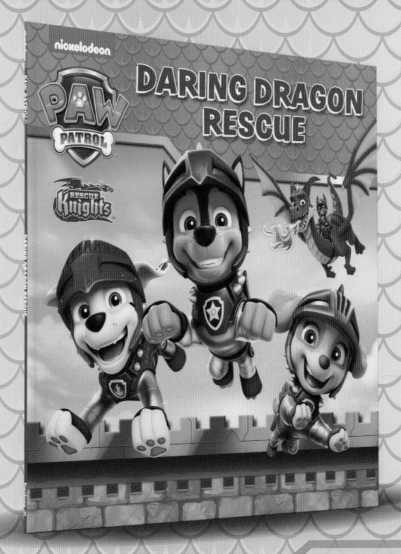

Have an adventure with the brave **Rescue Knights** as they save some stolen dragons in **DARING DRAGON RESCUE!**

ISBN: 978-0-00-853405-9